Bury Your Demons
A Short Story
By Timothy King

Copyright © 2024 by Timothy King

All rights reserved.

No portion of this book may be reproduced in any form without written permission from the publisher or author, except as permitted by U.S. copyright law.

This is a work of fiction. Any resemblance to real people or places is unintentional and used fictiously.

Trigger Warning

I tend to write violent and socially taboo stories.

This story contains:

Murder

Filicide

Sexually Explicit Scenes

Police Violence

and Overall Rough Shit...

Read at your own risk.

Foreward

From The Author

I originally wrote this story with the intention of including it in a future anthology. Hell, I still might, but something about this story really hit home for me. Anyone who has read my prior works might have noticed I tend to focus on a father's point of view. Well, that is because I am a father. This comes with all the fears and stressors that men have experienced since the dawn of time. Everything from fear of failure to the fear of losing a child weighs on men everywhere. This short story was an outlet for some of those fears, and it warped into something...more. I felt the need to get it out into the world as fast as possible. So, I hope you enjoy sharing in my trauma and fears.

Thank you for giving my short story a chance!

Contents

1. Bury Your Demons   1
2. About The Author   19
3. Other Works   21

Bury Your Demons

Keith paced back and forth, wearing a short trail into the living room carpet. His hands pressed against the sides of his head, trying to relieve the throbbing tension in his temples. Pain radiated outward from his sore chest and his eyes burned from the copious amount of tears he had shed.

"No. No. No." He muttered as he walked. His head shook subtly back and forth. The tension in his temples seemed to spread at an alarming rate. He began moving his hands erratically around his head, massaging different pressure points, desperate for any relief.

Susan sat completely still on the couch, her face expressionless. Her unkempt blonde hair covered one of her eyes, and a dark red stained her previously white blouse. She sat upright with her ankles crossed and her hands placed delicately on her knees. Her perfect posture sent a ripple of anger coursing through Keith's body. The sheer absurdity of it all infuriated him.

He exploded outward from his well-worn path and grabbed her by the shoulders. Despite his strong grip digging deep into her skin, Susan didn't react. She allowed him to shake her, her head rattling back and forth.

"Why? Why would you do it?" He screamed. Spittle flew from his mouth and coated her face with specks of moisture. "You stupid fucking bitch. How could you?" His face morphed into a deep shade of red. Hatred flared in his eyes. He released her and ran his fingers through his hair. "Oh, God!" In one swift motion, he grabbed the coffee table and flipped it. Magazines and the TV remote flew across the room. Turning back toward his wife he leaned in until his nose was touching hers, summoned a barbaric cry full of anguish, and unleashed it upon her. He continued yelling until there was no more air in his lungs. Weakness flooded his body and he crumpled to his knees in front of her. He lowered his head in defeat. With the last of his strength, he punched the couch. The wood in the armrest gave way and a loud crack filled the air. "How could you?" He cried quietly.

Sensing the fight draining from her husband, Susan reached out slowly, like a child giving a treat to a stranger's dog. When he didn't lash out, she rested her hand on his head. Her fingers weaved themselves through his thick black hair. Keith allowed her to caress him ever so gently, embracing the only good feeling he was experiencing at the moment. More sobs welled up in his throat, threatening to launch him into another inconsolable fit.

"Keith." Susan's voice was entirely void of emotion. "Keith, look at me." She commanded. Slowly, he obeyed, raising his eyes to meet his wife's callous gaze. "You need to pull yourself together. We have to clean this up."

Keith couldn't comprehend what she was saying. His head snapped toward the kitchen, where a pool of blood was slowly carving a path down the tile and soaking into the living room carpet. Little gray toes poked out from around the corner. Images of playing "this little piggie" with his daughter flashed in his mind, causing a wave of physical pain to tear through his body at the realization that he would never play those silly little games with his baby girl again. A weak moan escaped his lips.

"I did what I had to do." She said. "That," she extended one trembling finger toward the kitchen. "Was not our baby girl. That was something else. Something evil."

"You crazy bitch." He muttered.

"Maybe," she replied, "but you're going to help me clean this up. I am your wife, and I did the right thing. Now stand up and go out to the shed." Her bony finger drifted toward the back door. "Dig a hole in the backyard. We have to bury the body." She wrapped her hand around his chin and yanked hard, forcing him to meet her eyes. "Do you understand?"

Reluctantly, he nodded his head and pushed himself to his feet. Shuffling toward the back door, he was careful to avert his eyes from the massacred remains of his baby girl resting in the kitchen. Keith knew that seeing her would destroy him completely. He wouldn't be able to function, let alone dig a hole.

The evening air nipped at the exposed skin on his arms, neck, and head. Goosebumps broke out down his spine. Despite the late hour, the moon illuminated the backyard. He pushed through the discomfort of the chilly night and retrieved the shovel from the shed. Walking across the yard, he embedded the head of the shovel into the ground a few times, searching for a patch of soft dirt. He found one a few feet from the six-foot privacy fence that marked the boundary of his property. Sucking in a deep breath, he plunged the shovel into the ground.

Losing all track of time, he dug away. The muscles in his lower back screamed in agony with every swing of the dirt-filled shovel. The skin of his soft, uncallused hands tore against the rough wood of the shovel's handle. Blood trickled down his arms and dripped into the unconsecrated ground at his feet. He continued digging until he was standing almost shoulder-deep in the earth. Even then, it was only his wife's voice that snapped him out of his trance.

"That's deep enough." She said.

Keith looked around at the enormous hole he had dug, then down at his ruined hands. He tossed the shovel onto the lawn above him and climbed out.

A chill ran through his body at the sight of his wife. She was completely nude. Dried blood coated her body. Her blood-stained clothes sat in a pile at her feet. Without a word, she kicked them into the hole.

Susan stared at Keith expectantly until he relented and pulled off his shirt. He held it loosely in his outstretched hand, allowing it to slide out of his grasp and into the hole. As he slid his pants off, she moved past him and back toward the house. "I'll need your help moving the body." She called back to him.

Burning tears stung his eyes as he tossed his pants into the hole. His legs threatened to give out on him with each shaky step across the yard, until he reached the back door. He leaned against the door frame. Fighting off the imminent panic attack, he sucked in a deep breath and looked into the kitchen.

There, he saw a nude, blood-soaked Susan rolling their little girl into the rug from the dining room. Charlotte's eyes stared at him, void of life. Her slack expression ripped a hole in his soul and seared itself in his memory. He knew at that moment that he would never recover from this. Her tattered throat and soulless eyes would haunt his nightmares forever.

Susan didn't seem to be bothered by it. She simply continued rolling Charlotte up in the rug until the body was completely consumed, and the only thing visible were those cold, gray toes.

"How does that not bother you?" Keith asked incredulously.

Susan stood up, shaking her head. "Because it's not our daughter. It's something else. I knew something was wrong when she started hanging out with that new friend at school." a single tear escaped from the corner of her eye. She quickly wiped it away, smearing blood across her cheek. Shaking her head as if to shake away the emotions, she pointed to the rolled-up carpet. "Pick it up and bury it." She turned to the sink and turned on the water. "I'll finish cleaning up in here."

Reluctantly, Keith stepped forward and grabbed the rug with both hands. He yanked it toward himself. The rough material tore at the cuts and dried blood on his ragged hands. Straining against the dead weight, he managed to wrestle the carpet onto his shoulder. Charlotte never seemed heavy to him before. He recalled throwing her into the air a few days ago, but inside that rug, the seven-year-old's weight was bone-crushing. Keith carefully walked through the back door and continued his labored journey across the yard. Tears poured from his face with every step.

When he reached the hole, he froze. He knew what he had to do but couldn't bring himself to do it. He stood there staring into the darkness at his feet. Thoughts of his daughter being trapped down there ran through his head. He pictured her decaying corpse being devoured by worms and bugs. He must have been standing there for some time because Susan's shrill voice interrupted his morbid thoughts.

"You haven't buried her yet?" She appeared at his side and tossed several blood-soaked towels into the hole. "We don't have long before the sun rises."

"I don't know if I can do it." He whispered. Charlotte's dead weight bore down on his shoulder like the last hug he would ever receive from his daughter.

"Do you want me to go to prison?" She asked, throwing her hands up at her sides. "They won't understand, Keith! They won't believe that she was a monster!"

"That's because she wasn't!" He screamed. "She was our little girl, you fucking bitch." In a fit of anger, he pivoted and released his hold on the body. The bundle collapsed into the hole with a heartbreaking thud. Keith rushed around the hole to retrieve his shovel. He couldn't drag this out; he didn't trust himself to start again if he paused. As quickly as he could, he shoveled. "Is this what you want?" He shouted as he threw heaps of dark soil onto his daughter's body. "You want her gone so fucking bad?" He shouted incoherent sentences and obscenities as he tossed dirt into the hole. Keith worked hard, not stopping for a moment until he had completely filled in the hole, burying his sins.

He tossed the shovel aside and collapsed to the ground, sobbing. Slowly, Susan came to his side and dropped to her knees. She wrapped her arms around him while he cried. The feel of her nude skin on his caused his stomach to churn in revolt. He wanted to run, wanted to call the police, wanted to kill her. But he didn't. He sat there crying for a long time and she held him. They sat huddled like that until the first rays of sunlight broke through the trees at the back of their property.

"We have to shower." She whispered. "We can't let anyone see us like this." Her hands slid off his shoulders. She stood up and held out a hand for him to take.

His eyes drifted back to the loose dirt now covering his little girl, then back to his wife. She reached out and grabbed his hand, coaxing him to his feet. Keith allowed his wife to guide him through the yard and into the house. They paused at the front door so Susan could wash his feet with a wet cloth. She mumbled something about tracking mud into her clean house but Keith wasn't listening anymore. His shattered mind drifted to memories of happier times, his subconscious shielding him from his present reality.

Susan pulled him into the house and pulled the back door closed behind them. She tenderly led him up the stairs and down the hall toward their bedroom. Keith froze as they passed Charlotte's room, yanking his hand away from his wife's. Charlotte's door was cracked open and rays of sunlight leaked through the open window. Susan grabbed the door handle to pull it closed, but out of the corner of his eye, Keith saw the outline of a little girl looking out the window into the backyard. His heart exploded in his chest. He shoved his wife away from the room and smashed into the door with his shoulder. The door crashed into the wall behind it, bouncing back and nearly ripping off his toenail as he entered.

"Charlotte!" He shouted, then froze just inside the door. There was nobody there. His eyes darted wildly around the room, searching desperately for the little girl he had seen."Charlotte?" He pleaded.

Susan's grip on his shoulder caused him to jump.

"She's not in here, Keith." Susan whispered. "Come on." She slid her arm around his shoulders. Susan finished leading Keith down the hallway and into their bathroom. Steam radiated from the walk-in shower. Keith stood submerged in the scalding water, letting it wash away the dirt and shame. His skin turned an angry red from the unrelenting heat. Susan's fingers caressed his arms and back, helping to rid him of the grime. She reached around his body, using her soapy hands to wash his stomach. Her hands drifted lower, teasing at his groin. Her fingers reached his manhood and wrapped around it. He sucked in a deep breath and allowed his head to roll back. He stiffened against her hand as her stroke gained speed. For a few seconds all of the bad in his life washed away. He was about to lose himself to the excitement when the image of his dead daughter flashed in his mind. Everything came flooding back and he slapped her hand away.

"What're you doing?" He snapped.

She rested her cheek against his shoulder. "Just trying to take your mind off everything." She whispered.

Another surge of rage flooded through his body. Keith slowly turned around to face his wife, stifling the urge to smash her head into the bathroom tiles. Her emotionless eyes stared back at him, making it that much harder to restrain himself. "I really need to understand." He said.

Susan lowered her eyes. "You know why." She said firmly. "That wasn't our little girl anymore. I don't know how many times I have to say it." She reached past Keith and turned off the water. Stepping out of the shower, she grabbed a towel and dried her hair. Without looking at Keith, she added, "I did the right thing." She quickly wrapped the towel around herself and disappeared into their bedroom.

Keith stepped out of the shower, his hands shaking uncontrollably. Nausea broiled in his stomach. He tried to fight it back, but the acid liquid burned the back of his throat. He tossed open the toilet bowl and vomited into it. He threw up two more times before the nausea subsided. The muscles in his lower back cramped painfully and he slumped to the ground next to the toilet. Not bothering to get up, he reached around blindly on the counter and pulled down his towel before quickly drying himself off. Using the toilet for support, he hoisted himself to his feet and staggered out of the bathroom.

Susan was already in her spot on the right side of the bed, facing away from him. Her nude shoulders rose and fell rhythmically with her breathing. He clenched his fists. A bolt of anger tore through him. How could she do it? He knew Charlotte had been acting strange lately, but that was no excuse. If anything, the poor girl was sick. Instead of getting her help, the one person who was supposed to protect her tore her throat out in a vicious fashion. He wanted to wrap his tattered hands around Susan's neck and squeeze the life from her. He wanted to see the look in her eyes as the realization that she was dying set in. The image of his daughter's eyes staring at him as his wife rolled her body into the rug flashed in his mind and he wondered if his wife would have the same, cold look.

Keith inhaled deeply and unclasped his fists. The exhaustion was wearing him down, and he couldn't think straight. He shook the images from his mind, breathing slowly a few more times to compose himself. Giving into the drowsiness, he collapsed onto his side of the bed and drifted off to sleep.

"This little piggy went to market."

Keith awoke with a start when someone yanked on his big toe. He tried to sit up but some unseen force pressed him firmly into the bed. The midday sun streaming through their bedroom windows burned his retinas, forcing him to squint his eyes against the blinding light.

"This little piggy stayed home."

Icy fingers squeezed the next toe tightly. Keith's blood ran cold. The voice was hollow and monotone, a mockery of a little girl's voice. He forced his eyes open and couldn't believe what he saw.

Standing at the foot of his bed was Charlotte. Thick clumps of mud clung to her hair. The gashes in her throat seeped blood that ran down her chest in grotesque rivers. It coagulated into a disgusting soup at her feet.

"Charlotte?" He croaked.

"This little piggy had roast beef." Her fingers drifted to the third toe on his right foot. His eyes darted to the side to see his wife sleeping with her back to him.

Keith tried to sit up again, but that same invisible weight pinned him to the bed.

"This little piggy had none." The hollow, lifeless voice of his daughter rang out.

"Charlotte, baby, I'm so sorry." Tears carved a path through the stubble on his face. "I should've done more to help you. I should've stopped her."

A smile stretched across Charlotte's face. The sickly gray tint of her skin caused Keith's stomach to lurch, but he kept his eyes trained on his little girl.

"This little piggy went wee, wee, wee all the way home." With unnatural speed and precision, her hand darted out and gripped the pinky toe on his right foot and twisted. Agonizing pain tore through Keith's leg. He screamed and thrashed against his invisible restraints. His eyes clenched shut involuntarily as the warm sensation of his own blood spurted from the wound. When he looked back at Charlotte, she held his pinky toe between two fingers for him to see. She wiggled it back and forth.

"Susan!" Keith shrieked. "Susan, wake up!"

Charlotte laughed. "Susan!" She mimicked his voice nearly perfectly. "Susan, wake up!" She giggled. Charlotte's corpse launched the severed toe at her father. It smacked against Keith's cheek with a meaty thud. His chest rose and fell in rapid succession.

"My cunt of a mother won't wake up." Charlotte crept around the side of the bed until she was next to Susan. Slowly, she reached out and pushed on the woman's shoulder.

Susan's head lulled to the side, her eyes stretched open in terror. Keith's eyes drifted down to her neck and his mouth gaped wide. He tried to scream, but only a squeak came out. His wife's neck was torn open, revealing jagged chunks of white bone. The lacerations were deep enough to nearly decapitate her. Susan's head hung on by a few patches of stringy skin.

Keith thrashed against invisible restraints, fighting with every fiber of his being to reach out to his apparently dead wife.

Standing next to Susan's nearly headless body, Charlotte laughed. Her laughter grew harder and harder with every second until the monstrosity hunched over, gasping for air.

"What's so fucking funny?" Keith shouted.

Charlotte stopped laughing. She lifted her head and smiled at her father. One of her cold hands snapped out and grabbed Susan's shoulder. With one tug, she rolled the corpse onto the floor. Hopping over Susan, the Charlotte creature climbed into the bed. Her hair fell wildly around her face. It tickled Keith's nose as she leaned in close. Charlotte pressed her lips to her father's ears.

"Mommy was right." Keith willed himself to move but could not even lift a finger. Charlotte grabbed onto the wall behind the headboard and sunk her fingers into the drywall. She hoisted herself up, climbing the wall like a spider until she dangled from the roof. Her head snapped backward, a sickening crunch reverberating through the room. Muddy clumps of blood and tissue fell from the open wound in her neck, covering him in gore. "I'm not your little girl." The creature that looked like Charlotte smiled. "I ripped her to pieces in the woods."

"No! I'll fucking kill you!" He shouted. Spittle flew from his lips. The muscles in his neck strained, the veins bulging under his skin. "I'll fucking kill you!"

The Charlotte creature dropped back onto the bed with a thud. It stepped over Keith's stomach and straddled him.

In a perfect imitation of his daughter, the creature cried. Tears poured down its face. "You already did that, Daddy. Don't you remember?" She lowered her head, and her long, mud-caked hair obscured her face. "You buried me." The voice mockery slipped away with the word 'me', and the undead creature's own baritone reverberated off the walls of the room.

"Why are you doing this?" He shouted.

It snapped its head back up. "Because I can." It whispered. The Charlotte thing walked two fingers up Keith's chest. They stopped at the soft patch of flesh between the collarbones. Charlotte's warped and horrific visage leaned in close, their noses nearly touching. The decaying stench of his daughter's corpse permeated Keith's nostrils. Slowly, the Charlotte demon applied pressure to the tender flesh at the base of his neck. It was uncomfortable at first, then morphed into agony as the fingers broke through the flesh. Heat rushed around his neck and shoulders as blood seeped from the open wound.

Keith screamed out in pain, but the approaching sound of a police siren drowned out his cries. Charlotte's head snapped in the direction of the bedroom door.

"Looks like playtime is over." The creature hissed. It rolled off the bed, collapsing to the floor with a thud.

Keith sucked in a deep breath. He sat up in bed, finally able to move freely. Throwing the covers aside, he exposed his nude, blood-soaked body to the cold night air.

Keith hurled himself off the bed and to his wife's side. Hot tears poured from his eyes, and snot bubbled from his nose. He allowed himself to collapse against the wall and was resting his head in his hands when something bright caught his eyes.

Reaching under the bed to retrieve the object, he quickly realized it was Susan's cell phone. Turning it over, he saw it was open to a text thread with Susan's mother. The last text from Susan read, "Send help. Keith killed Charlotte."

Keith's blood froze in his body. Nausea rumbled and threatened to spew over. The sirens were in his front yard now, creating an ear-shattering howl. The sound of the front door to the house exploding open rang out. A series of voices started shouting from downstairs. He could make out phrases like "sheriff's office" and "show yourself."

The phone slipped from his hand and shattered against the tile floor. Susan's blood coated the phone, seeping into the cracks until the screen went out. Keith slipped into a state of delirium. A laugh crept up his throat. It started as a smirk, then a light chuckle. Finally, it grew to a ridiculous bellowing cackle.

A few seconds later, the door to his bedroom burst open and three cops piled into the room, pistols drawn. There was a series of incomprehensible shouts coming from the officers. Keith locked eyes with Charlotte's deceased corpse.

A smirk wormed its way onto her face as an officer slammed Keith's face down into the tile. The smirk grew bigger when the officer ruthlessly snapped the handcuffs into place.

Just as the officers prepared to drag him from the room, Charlotte winked.

About The Author

Timothy King is an adult horror author who enjoys delving into the complexities of human nature. When he is not writing spine-chilling tales, he is spending time with his wife and kids in beautiful Tampa, Florida.

You can find him on Facebook, Tiktok or by emailing him at:

Timothykingauthor@gmail.com

If you enjoyed this book, please consider leaving a review on Amazon or Goodreads!

Other Works

Novels:

Seven Rabbits

Short Stories:

Bad Book Boogie (located in the Splatter Chatter Anthology, Volume One)

Made in the USA
Columbia, SC
24 September 2024